Written by Judy Erb

Illustrated by Emily Allen

Bookbaby Publishers

Being Me Is the Best Thing to Be

ISBN 978-1-66780-427-9

For all the students who I enjoyed reading to-
may you know that being yourself really is the best thing to be.

To Mark-without your love and support
Honey would have never hatched.

On a crisp autumn afternoon, Mama Turtle is spending her day on the bank of a lake with her daughter, Honey.

Together they enjoy the cool breeze and bright sunshine.

A busy beaver slaps her tail on the water to warn her family of danger. The noise is as piercing as a clap of thunder.

"Mama, I wish I could make a loud sound like that when I leave a log and enter the water. I only make a soft splashing sound."

"Honey, slipping into the water quietly lets you hide from other animals. That beaver spends every day building a dam to hide in and can't soak up the sunshine like you do."

An egret glides through the air smoothly, sailing over their heads.

“Mama, I wish I could fly. I would go as high as I could and dive down to grab fish out of the water. Wouldn’t that be wonderful?”

“Honey, your shell is too heavy for you to fly. Most animals cannot take their homes with them like you do.”

A gray fox lurks behind some bushes listening for small animals.

"Mama, look at that fox's ears. If I had ears that big, I could hear things from far away!"

“Honey, your ears are waterproof, which is much better for swimming. That fox can't enjoy the water like you do.”

While the turtles take a dip in the lake, the sun tickles a fish making its bright colors shimmer.

Blue-green and yellow-green blend
into a pink band of color that
stretches along the fish's side.

"Mama, look at the dazzling colors on that fish. Having such beautiful colors is a special way to go through life."

“Honey, those colors make it easy to see, which makes it hard for that fish to hide from big fish who chase her. She doesn't blend in like you do."

A woodpecker peck-peck-pecks at a tree looking for food and building herself a home.

“Oh, Mama, if we made our home in a tree, we could look around and see everything from above. What a terrific view we would have!”

"Honey, if you lived high in a tree, it would be hard to climb down. You might fall and crack your shell. That bird can't live in the water like you do."

When it gets close to dark, Honey grows tired from all the walking and swimming she has done. Not far away, a sleepy black bear prepares to hibernate for the winter.

"Mama, if I could rest all winter like that bear, I would feel so refreshed when I woke up."

“Honey, if you stayed in a den all winter like that bear, you would miss how magnificent everything looks in the snow. You would miss the sun glistening through the ice. That bear can't enjoy winter like you do."

Honey and Mama fall asleep in the cool mud along the edge of the lake.

Honey dreams of all the animals she saw that day.

In the morning, Honey wakes up happy.

"Mama, I have decided that a turtle like me is the **BEST THING TO BE!**"

***Being Me Is the Best Thing to Be* is Judy Erb's first book.** She is a retired educator who enjoyed teaching students from kindergarten through fifth grade for thirty-three years. During her career, Judy received recognition for her teaching, and she was given the opportunity to learn at Harvard University in the Project Zero program studying with Howard Gardener. Judy also spent time at Columbia University where she studied best practices for teaching reading and writing to children. Her favorite thing about teaching has always been reading to children and discussing books with them. Judy loves to travel, read, and spend time at her home in the North Carolina mountains with her husband and their fur babies.

Please check out Judy's website: www.judyerbauthor.com

Emily Allen is an up-and-coming independent artist, studying Studio Art and Psychology at Appalachian State University. Though mainly an oil painter, Emily can bring life to any medium through her unique use of color and texture. Her passion and inspiration for art come from life's simple beauties: the sounds of seafoam; the sight of sunlight seeping through a treetop. As per the artist: "There is so much in this wonderfully wide world to explore, and I hope to bring its whimsy to your fingertips every time you touch my work!".

More of Emily's work available for viewing: https://instagram.com/simplyroseyart/